LiTTLE BAT

in night school

CALDECOTT HONOR WINNER AND *NEW YORK TIMES* BESTSELLER
BRIAN LIES

HOUGHTON MIFFLIN HARCOURT
BOSTON   NEW YORK

To teachers, who bring light to the darkness

All rights reserved. For information about permission to reproduce selections from this book, write to trade.permissions@hmhco.com or to Permissions, Houghton Mifflin Harcourt Publishing Company, 3 Park Avenue, 19th Floor, New York, New York 10016.

hmhbooks.com

The illustrations in this book were done with acrylic and watercolor paints and colored pencil on Strathmore paper.
The text was set in Adobe Garamond Pro.
Design by Natalie Fondriest

Library of Congress Cataloging-in-Publication Data is on file.

ISBN: 978-0-358-26984-7

Manufactured in China
SCP 10 9 8 7 6 5 4 3 2 1
4500820708

Little Bat was *ready*. He had everything he needed . . .

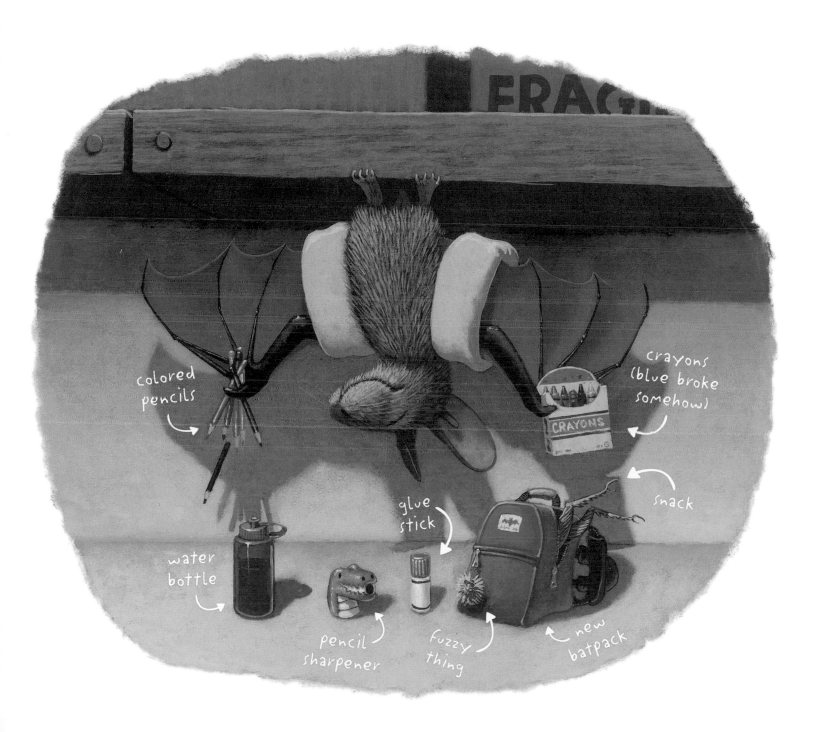

. . . except maybe some patience.

When is sunset?

Is it time to go yet?

How about now?

Now??

School is
going to be
so much fun!

How about
now?

I can't wait
to meet the
other bats!

"Shhh," Mama Bat yawned, awakened
for the hundredth time. *"Rest."*

When night fell and they finally arrived at school,
it was bigger than Little Bat had expected.

"Well, hello!" The teacher smiled at him. "I'm
Ms. C."

In the classroom, Little Bat saw a pair
of raccoons, some owlets, and a ferret.
Where were the other bats?

There they were—over by that wall!
He let out his breath.

"Hi," he said. "I'm Little Bat. Want to play?"

"We're already playing—" one said.
"—with each other," the other added.

Little Bat flew into a cubby to hide, but someone
else was already there.

"Hi—what are you doing?" he asked.

"I'm just . . . hanging out," she replied.

"Oh," Little Bat said. "Is it okay if I hang out
here too?"

"I guess so," she said. "But why aren't you out
there with *them?*"

"I don't know anybody," Little Bat sighed.
"I want to go home."

"Me too," she said. "I'm Ophelia."

"I'm Little Bat." He blinked. "Hey, now
we *do* know somebody here!"

"Circle time," Ms. C. called. "Everyone gather 'round!"
She flicked on more lights.

"Guess we have to join them." Little Bat jumped.
"Wait—bats explode in light!" Ophelia cried.

Little Bat laughed. "That's just a myth. I'll
go if you will!"
"Deal!" Ophelia agreed.

Little Bat and Ophelia stuck together. Ms. C. taught them to sing "The Seals on the Bus." They talked about the patterns the stars make and why the moon changes shape.

Then it was time for show-and-tell.

I brought a car. You copied me.

I brought a car. No, you copied me.

I've got half of a Popsicle stick!

I've got the other half!

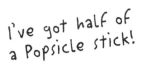

I have a bumbershoot!

We found this in someone's backyard!

Little Bat hadn't brought anything to share, so he held his wings wide. "These are my floaties," he announced.

The others gasped. "Do they help you fly? Do they keep you warm?"

He shrugged. "No, I just like them."

"Neat!" the others said.

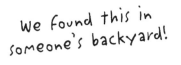

I like cephalopods!

During math, they practiced counting.

"*Psst*—turn it around," Ophelia whispered.
"Oops!" Little Bat laughed.

At nap time, everyone found a comfy place to rest.

Then it was time for art. Little Bat
threw himself into making prints.

He loved the feel of the squishy clay.

But Little Bat looked up and saw what someone
else was making. "I stink at art," he cried. "I quit!"

"Hey, don't get upset," the ferret said. "I've been doing this a lot longer than you. And you know, practice makes—"

"—*perfect*," Little Bat and Ophelia groaned.

"No, practice makes *better!*" the ferret said. "Everyone can get better. That's what makes it exciting!"

"I guess I *could* try again," Little Bat said.

At munch time, Ophelia held something out. "This is delicious—my mama found it on the road. Want some?"

"Um, no, thank you," Little Bat said. "But I'm glad you like it."

He pushed the straw into his juice, and it squirted. He grinned and squeezed it again, harder.

Hey!

"I'm *so* sorry!" Little Bat cried. "I didn't mean for that to happen!"

Ms. C. leaned in. "It's kind of you to help clean up," she said.

It WAS kind of funny.

"Time for recess," Ms. C. announced.
"What do you want us to do?" they asked.
"Use your imagination!" she replied.

"Recess is boring!" a raccoon groaned.

"But look at all this great stuff!" Little Bat pointed. "I bet we could build something."

They got busy.

The two other bats came over.

"Can we help—" one started.

"—with what you're making?" the other finished.

"Of course," Little Bat said. "Grab something to add!"

The round rug made a perfect racetrack.

"Story time," Ms. C. called.

Everyone grumbled. "Awww—we were just getting started!"

But they gathered around as Ms. C. opened a book and took them far back into the past. *Could the heroes escape before the time door closed, trapping them forever?* As the pterosaurs gained on them . . . a ray of morning light fell across the pages.

"Annnd . . . we'll have to leave it there for now,"
Ms. C. said.
"NO!" everyone pleaded. "Just a little more!"
"Don't worry, the story will wait for us."
Ms. C. smiled. "Time to gather your things."

"That was a pretty good night after all," Little Bat
remarked. "Are you coming back again tonight?"
    "I will if you do," Ophelia said.
    "Deal!" he agreed.

Little Bat leapt out into the air, his head buzzing with all he had learned.
   He couldn't *wait* to be back in night school.

You won't believe what my friends eat!

My best friend likes to hang upside down too!

There's a song I can teach you!

Somebody almost got in trouble for spilling juice.

We read the most amazing story!

I know all my numbers now!

Did you know the moon doesn't actually get skinnier?